No foal yet.

NO FOAL YET

by Jessie Haas ◈ pictures by Jos. A. Smith

Greenwillow Books, New York

Watercolor paints, colored pencils, and watercolor pencils were used for the full-color art. The text type is Berkeley Oldstyle ITC.

Printed in Hong Kong by South China Printing Company (1988) Ltd. First Edition 10 9 8 7 6 5 4 3 2 1

Library of Congress Cataloging-in-Publication Data

Haas, Jessie.
No foal yet / by Jessie Haas ; pictures by Jos. A. Smith.
p. cm.
Summary: Nora and her grandparents wait for their mare Bonnie to have her foal.
ISBN 0-688-12925-0. ISBN 0-688-12926-9 (lib. bdg.)
[1. Horses—Fiction. 2. Animals—Infancy—Fiction.]
I. Smith, Jos. A. (Joseph Anthony) (date), ill. II. Title.
PZ7.H1129No 1995 [E]—dc20
94-6265 CIP AC

FOR HELEN CORSA
— J. H.

Me, too— S.C.H.

FOR KARI, JOE, EMILY, AND ANDREA—
SOME VERY SPECIAL PEOPLE
— J. A. S.

Bonnie is going to have a foal. Any day now. When Gramp unhitches at night, he says, "This is the last time I will plow with her."

Nora helps him make a bed of straw in Bonnie's stall. Then Gramp leads Bonnie inside and feeds her.

"Do you think she'll have the foal tonight?" asks Nora.

"I wouldn't be surprised," says Gramp. "We'll keep an eye on her, in case she needs help."

Before bed Gramp goes to the barn. Nora should be sleeping, but she watches from her upstairs window. She sees Gramp's flashlight cross the yard, and after a minute she sees it come back again.
No foal yet.

In the morning Nora runs out before breakfast. Bonnie turns her head and blows her sweet breath on Nora's face. Her sides are big and round. The foal is still inside her.

Nora tells about the foal in show-and-tell. The class can come to see it after it is born.

"When?" everybody asks.

"Maybe today," says Nora.

When Nora jumps off the school bus, she runs to the barn first. Even before her snack. Even before she takes off her shoes and socks to go barefoot in the grass.

But only Bonnie is in the stall, fat and patient.

"Take her out for a walk, Nora," Gramp says. "A little exercise might help." Nora leads Bonnie around the yard and up and down the road. Nora eats an apple, and Bonnie eats the core. But the foal doesn't come that day.

At night Nora sings in the school concert. Gramp has to stay home, in case the foal comes. But it doesn't.

The next night Gramp goes to a meeting, and Gram and Nora stay home. Gram goes out to the barn four times. Nora goes six times.

Bonnie blinks when they turn on the light. She is sleepy, and they keep waking her up.

Gramp sets his alarm clock for the middle of the night. At breakfast he yawns.

No foal yet.

Gram sets her bread to rise and walks out to the barn. When she puts the bread in the oven, she goes out again.

No foal.

In class everybody asks Nora, “Is it born yet?”

Nora has to say no.

Each afternoon Nora takes Bonnie out in the yard. Bonnie walks slowly. If Nora looks hard, she can see the foal moving. If she puts her hand on Bonnie's side, she can feel it kick. But it won't come out.

On Saturday Gramp is so tired from getting up at night that he falls asleep before supper. Gram puts the casserole in the oven and looks out the window. But her feet are tired from walking back and forth. She sits down in her rocking chair.

Nora starts toward the barn one more time. But the kittens are playing on the porch, and she stops to watch them.

Ting! goes the timer, and Gram takes out the casserole. She wakes up Gramp.

"I'll go check Bonnie," Nora calls.

When Nora comes into the barn, Bonnie nickers. Her voice is deep and special. Nora hurries to the stall.

Bonnie stands with her head down. She is licking something in the straw. Nora opens the door and slips inside.

In front of Bonnie is a little brown foal. Bonnie licks him all over. Her tongue swirls his damp hair.

"Oh, *Bonnie*!" Nora says. "He's beautiful!" She turns to go call Gram and Gramp. But the foal starts moving, and Nora has to watch.

The foal sticks his legs straight out in front. He sits up like a dog. Then he gets his hind legs up. He falls over on his nose in the straw, and Bonnie licks him again.

Nora feels Gramp's hand on her shoulder.

"Well, Bonnie," Gramp says, "you didn't need help after all."

The foal sticks his legs out again. Up goes his front end. Up goes his back end. He wobbles, and he staggers, and he stands! When he has stood a few minutes, he starts to walk. He doesn't pick his feet up. He just scuffs them through the straw. Back, back along Bonnie's side he goes, until he finds milk. He wags his curly tail, and he drinks.

"Can I touch him, Gramp?" asks Nora.

"Go ahead," says Gramp.

Nora pats Bonnie first. "*Good* girl, Bonnie!"

Then she touches the foal. His hair is soft and deep, like the fur of Nora's old teddy bear.

Gram comes to the stall door. When she sees the foal, she smiles. "*Finally*, he's come!" she says.

Nora pats the foal's rump. He wiggles his tail harder.

"That's what we're going to call him," Nora says. "Finally!"